MARY MIDDLING
AND OTHER SILLY FOLK
Nursery Rhymes and Nonsense Poems

by ROSE FYLEMAN

SELECTED BY NEIL PHILIP

Illustrated by Katja Bandlow

CLARION BOOKS
NEW YORK

Clarion Books
a Houghton Mifflin Company imprint
215 Park Avenue South, New York, NY 10003

Published in the United States in 2004 by arrangement with
The Albion Press Ltd., Spring Hill, Idbury, Oxfordshire OX7 6RU, England

The poems in this book were first published in 1931 in *Fifty-One New Nursery Rhymes* by Rose Fyleman,
which was published in the United States by Doubleday in 1932.

Copyright © 2004 by the Estate of Rose Fyleman
Illustrations copyright © 2004 by Katja Bandlow

Designed by Emma Bradford

The illustrations were drawn in Chinese ink, scanned, and colored in Adobe Photoshop.
The text was set in 15-point Weiss Bold.

For information about permission to reproduce selections from this book, write to
Permissions, Houghton Mifflin Company, 215 Park Avenue South, New York, NY 10003.

www.houghtonmifflinbooks.com

Library of Congress Cataloging-in-Publication Data

Fyleman, Rose, 1877-1957.
Mary Middling, and other silly folk nursery rhymes and
nonsense poems / by Rose Fyleman ; illustrated by Katja
Bandlow.
p. cm.
ISBN 0-618-38141-4
1. Children's poetry, English. 2. Nonsense verses,
English. 3. Nursery rhymes, English. [1. English poetry.
2. Nonsense verses. 3. Nursery rhymes.] I. Bandlow, Katja,
ill. II. Title.
PR6011.Y5A6 2004
821'.912-dc22
2003026751

ISBN-13: 978-0-618-38141-8
ISBN-10: 0-618-38141-4

10 9 8 7 6 5 4 3 2 1

Typesetting: Servis Filmsetting Ltd., Manchester
Color origination: Classicscan, Singapore
Printed in China by South China Printing Co.

THE WEATHERCOCK

The moon is like a lamp,
   The sun is like a fire,
The weathercock can see them both;
   He sits upon the spire.

He sits upon the spire
   High above the ground—
I'd like to be a weathercock,
   Turning round and round.

THE SMART LADY

There was an old lady who wore a great bonnet
With radishes, lettuce, and carrots upon it;
Folk smiled when they saw her thus oddly attired,
But she said, "How delightful to be so admired!"

MARY MIDDLING

Mary Middling had a pig,
Not very little and not very big,
Not very pink, not very green,
Not very dirty, not very clean,
Not very good, not very naughty,
Not very humble, not very haughty,
Not very thin, not very fat;
Now what would you give for a pig like that?

To Market

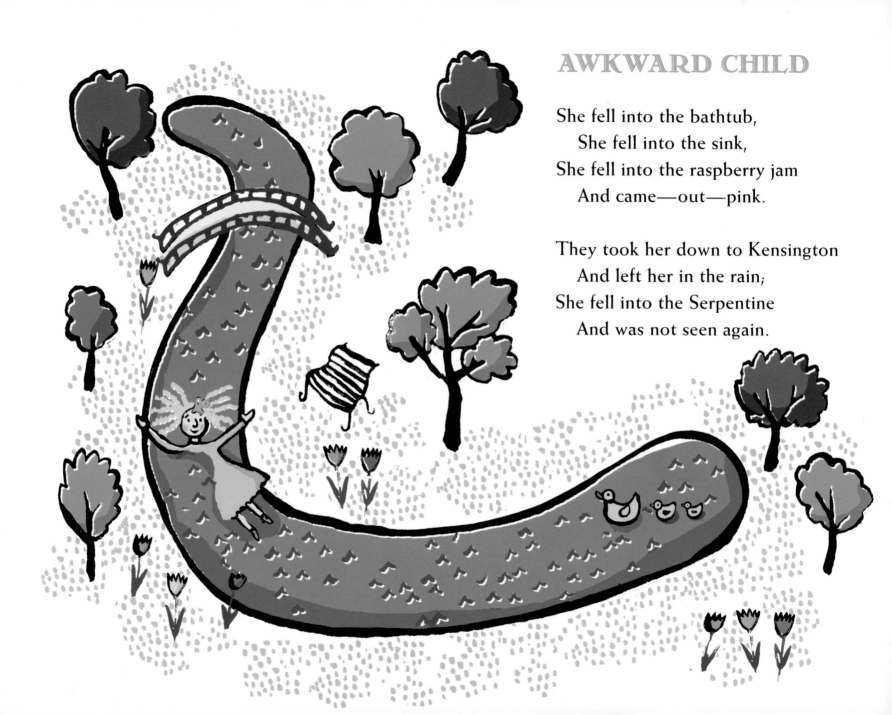

AWKWARD CHILD

She fell into the bathtub,
　　She fell into the sink,
She fell into the raspberry jam
　　And came—out—pink.

They took her down to Kensington
　　And left her in the rain;
She fell into the Serpentine
　　And was not seen again.

RATHER SILLY

There once was a man with a queer sort of notion
You could always be happy by keeping in motion;
He traveled all day upon buses and cars,
And hoarded the tickets in marmalade jars.

THE GREENWICH GENTLEMAN

There was a gentleman of Greenwich
Who lived on watercress and spinach;
But on his birthday, in July,
He had a slice of custard pie.

FUN

Deborah Dolores she liked a bit of fun,
She went to the baker's and bought a penny bun;
She dipped it in the treacle and threw it at her teacher;
Deborah Dolores she *was* a wicked creature.

THE COW

Meg Moriarty bought a cow,
She tried to milk it, but didn't know how;
She didn't know how, but she tried her best. . . .
Nobody seems to know the rest.

RABBIT

Rabbit!
You see a lettuce and you grab it.
It really is a very shocking habit,
Rabbit!

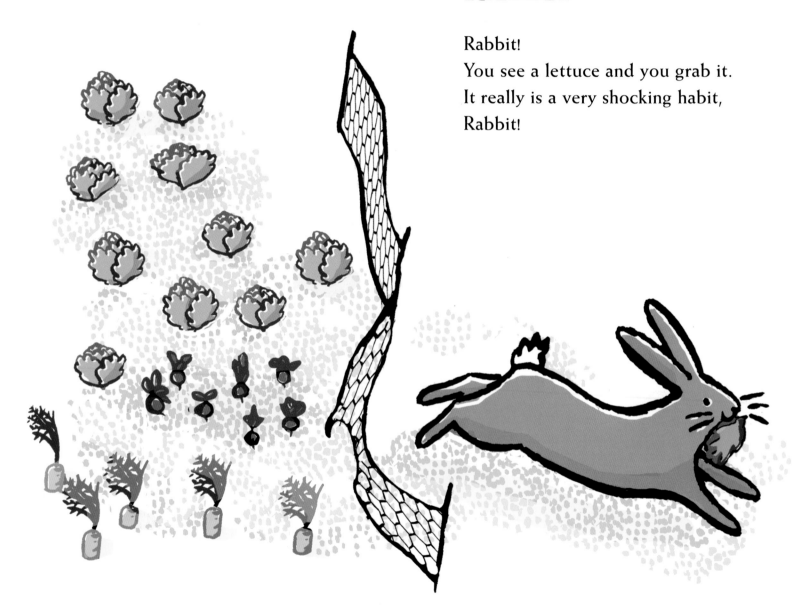

THE SPOTTED HORSE

I had a little spotted horse;
He had four legs and a tail, of course.
I gave him nuts and gingerbread
And crimson tassels for his head;
But I could never make him go;
The reason why I do not know.

CHRISTOPHER CORKER

Christopher Corker would never use a chair,
He stood upon his head with his legs in the air;
He stood like that for his dinner and his tea;
It might do for you—it would never do for me.

TOO BAD

Lanky Lawrence was so thin
That people took him for a pin;
But when he moved the other leg
They took him for a washing peg.

THE KING AND THE QUEEN

The Queen wore a silver crown,
   The King wore a gold one,
The Queen liked a gay new gown,
   The King liked an old one.

The King wore sensible shoes,
   The Queen wouldn't wear 'em.
The King liked oniony stews,
   The Queen couldn't bear 'em.

THE PIRATE

There was a pirate brave and bold
Who had a mug of solid gold,
And always when he went to sea
Drank turtle soup instead of tea;
But when he got on shore again
His meals were very neat and plain.

MICE

I think mice
Are rather nice.

Their tails are long,
Their faces small,
They haven't any
Chins at all.
Their ears are pink,
Their teeth are white,
They run about
The house at night.
They nibble things
They shouldn't touch
And no one seems
To like them much.

But *I* think mice
Are nice.

HEN'S SONG

Chick, chick, come out of your shell,
I've warmed you long and I've watched you well;
The sun is hot and the sky is blue,
Quick, chick, it's time you came through.

THE PAINTER

There once was a painter, and what do you think?
He painted his dog all yellow and pink;
They went for a walk on a fine summer's day
And all the folk shouted Hurray and Hurray.

MY DUCKY, MY DEARIE

My ducky, my dearie,
  If I had a crown
I'd hire a pony
  And ride into town;
I'd buy a balloon
  And a watering-can,
A sugary pig,
  And a gingerbread man.

WITCH, WITCH

"Witch, witch, where do you fly?" . . .
"Under the clouds and over the sky."

"Witch, witch, what do you eat?" . . .
"Little black apples from Hurricane Street."

"Witch, witch, what do you drink?" . . .
"Vinegar, blacking, and good red ink."

"Witch, witch, where do you sleep?" . . .
"Up in the clouds, where pillows are cheap."

THE DONKEY

My donkey has a bridle
    Hung with silver bells,
He feeds upon the thistles
    Growing on the fells.
The bells keep chiming, chiming
    A little silver song;
If ever I should lose him
    It would not be for long.